Author's Note

For decades Juan Bobo, the invention of rural storytellers of Puerto Rico, has been the most popular fictional character on the island. Although some of Juan Bobo's "noodlehead" behavior also occurs in the folklore of other countries, the oldest and best-known Juan Bobo stories authentically illustrate what life was like in poor rural areas of Puerto Rico at the beginning of the twentieth century.

In retelling a few of these old tales, I have used my own voice and have tried to preserve some of the rural Puerto Rican flavor.

—CTB-G

Illustrator's Note

Over the years, artists have drawn Juan Bobo in a variety of ways. I feel privileged to have been able to interpret how I see this beloved folk character in my imagination. Juan Bobo belongs to all Puerto Ricans and, one could say, to all people, for his spirit is universal. I hope my drawings help us to see that there is a bit of Juan Bobo in all of us—and that there is a bit of all of us in Juan Bobo.

—ERN

HarperCollins*Publishers*

An I Can Read Book®

JUAN BOBO

Four Folktales from Puerto Rico

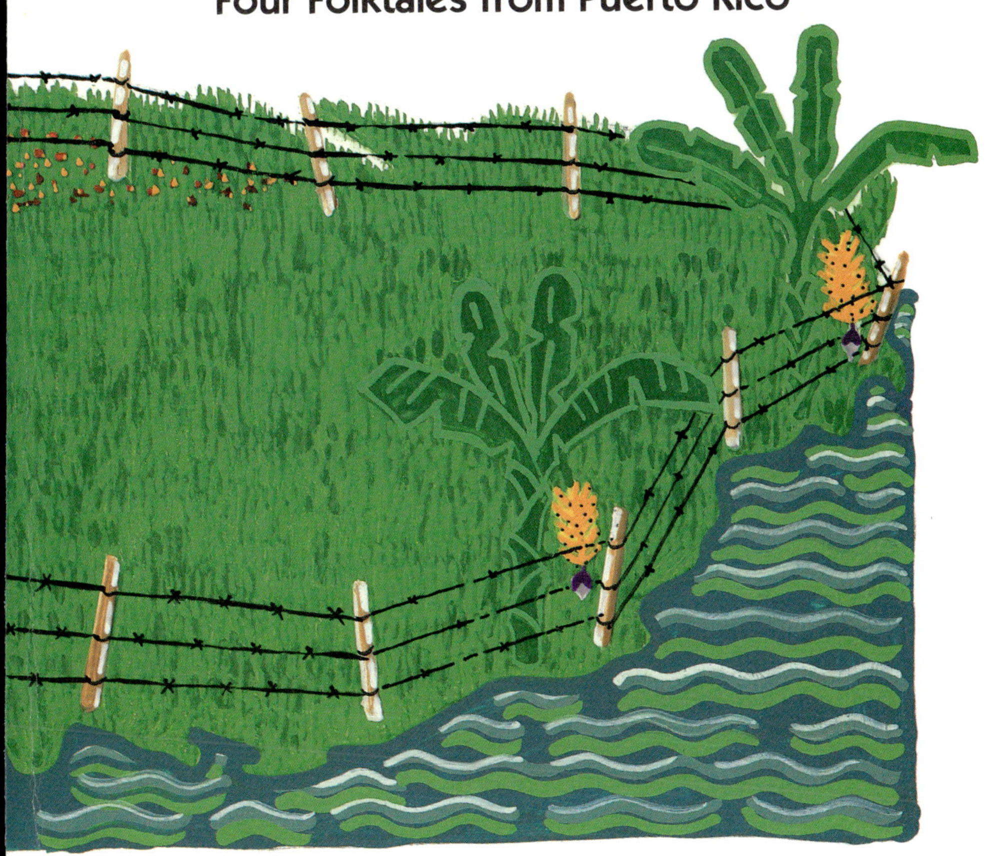

retold by Carmen T. Bernier-Grand
pictures by Ernesto Ramos Nieves

To Matthew, Juliana & Guillermo,
three *jibaritos* living in the United States,
and to Natasha who believes in Juan Bobo
—CTB-G

In gratitude to Pat Cummings, Robert Warren,
Jim Metzinger, Liz Bruce, Frances Goldin, Mildred Quinones,
Gigi Ramos, and to *my* "Mama," Fefa Nieves Colon,
who gave me life and my first art lessons
—ERN

Juan Bobo
Four Folktales from Puerto Rico

Library of Congress Cataloging-in-Publication Data
Bernier-Grand, Carmen T.
Juan Bobo : four folktales from Puerto Rico / retold by Carmen T. Bernier-Grand ; pictures by Ernesto Ramos Nieves.
p. cm. — (An I can read book)
Contents: The best way to carry water — A pig in Sunday clothes — Do not sneeze, do not scratch, do not eat — A dime a jug.
ISBN 0-06-023389-3. — ISBN 0-06-023390-7 (lib. bdg.)
1. Juan Bobo (Legendary character)—Juvenile literature. [1. Juan Bobo (Legendary character) 2. Folklore—Puerto Rico.] I. Ramos Nieves, Ernesto, ill. II. Title. III. Series.
PZ8.1.B4173Ju 1994 93-12936
398.21—dc20 CIP
[E] AC

1 2 3 4 5 6 7 8 9 10

First Edition

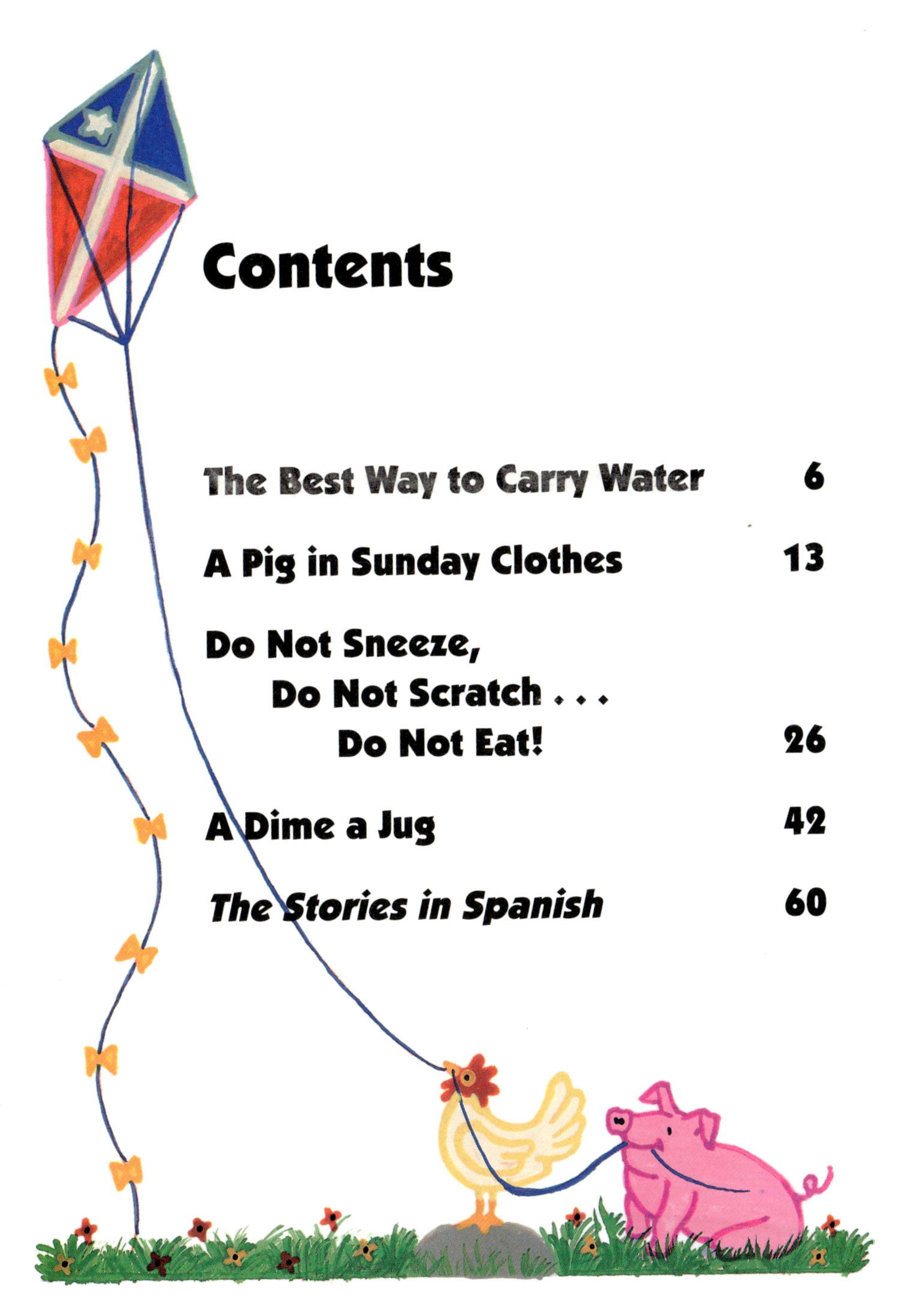

Contents

The Best Way to Carry Water

"Juan Bobo!" Mama called.

"Yes, Mama," said Juan Bobo.

"Please bring me some water

from the stream," said Mama.

"Ay!" cried Juan Bobo.

"Do I have to?"

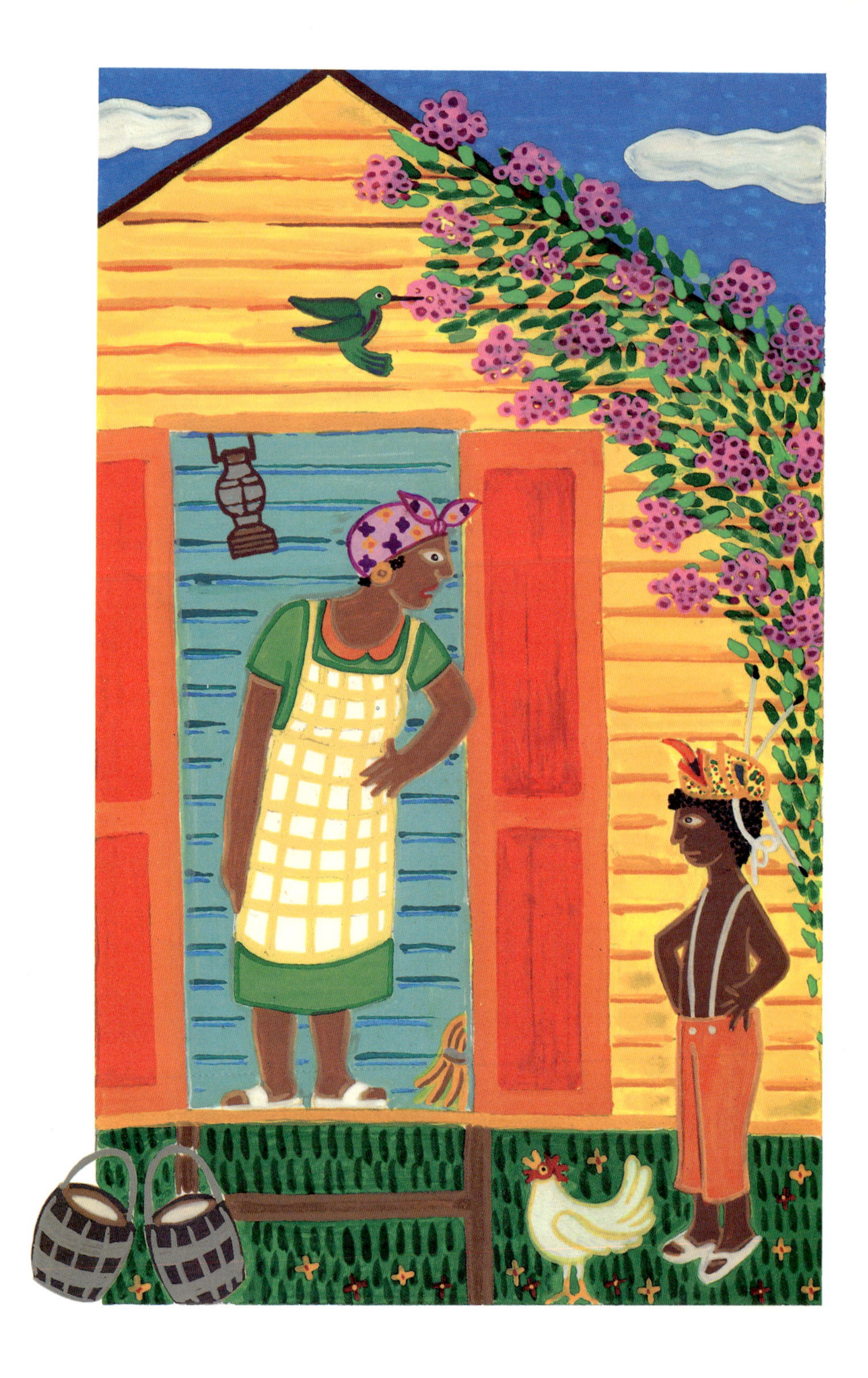

Mama dropped two empty buckets
outside the door.
"I need water to wash dishes,"
she said.
"Ay, Mama," said Juan Bobo.
"When those buckets are full,
they are too heavy to carry."
"Then use something else,"
said Mama,
"but bring me some water."
"Ay," said Juan Bobo.

Mama swept and dusted
the living room and the bedroom.
Then she went back into the kitchen.
"Juan Bobo, did you get me
the water?" she asked.
"Yes, Mama," said Juan Bobo.
"And guess what, Mama.
I think I am growing stronger!"
"Why?" said Mama.
"Because," said Juan Bobo,
"as I walked back from the stream,
the water felt lighter and lighter."
"That is odd," said Mama.

Then she stepped into a big puddle!

"Juan Bobo!

Is this the water you got me?"

"No, Mama!" said Juan Bobo.

"The water I got you

is in those two baskets."

A Pig in Sunday Clothes

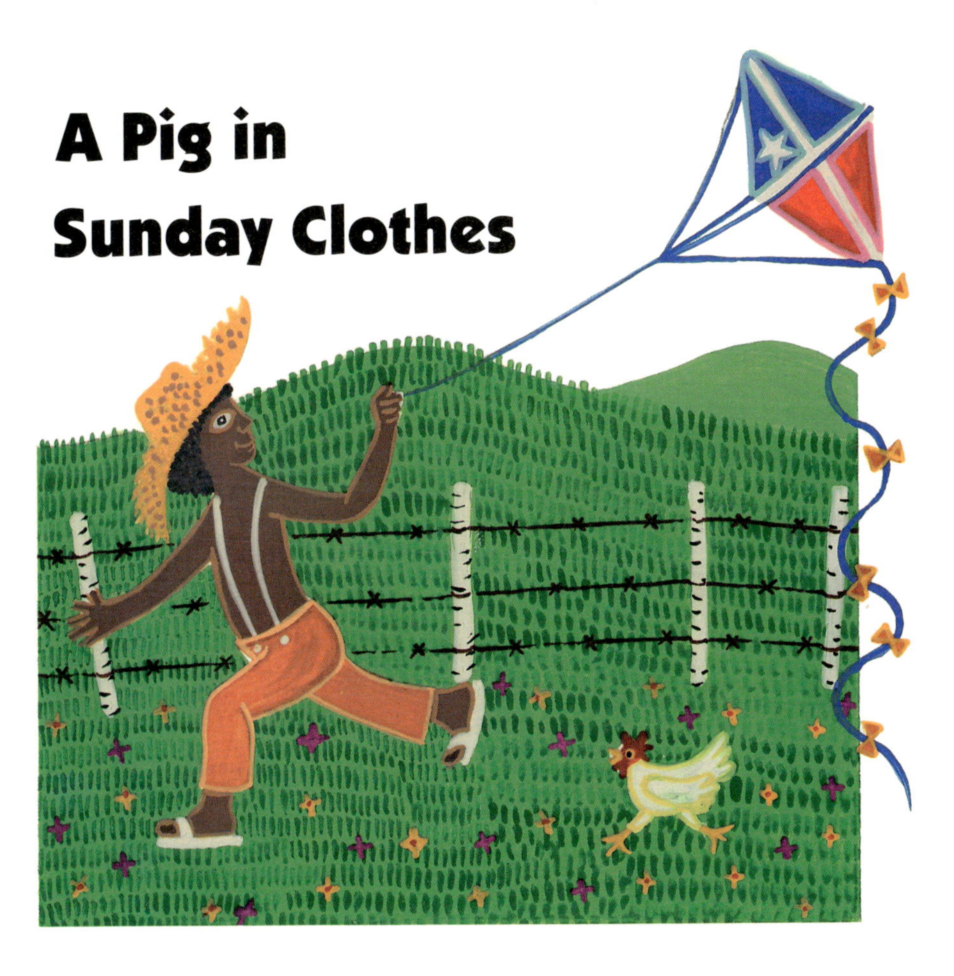

"Juan Bobo," Mama said.

"Either you come to church with me

or you take care of the pig."

"I will take care of the pig, Mama."

As soon as Mama left for church,

the pig began to squeal.

“Do you want to go to church?”

Juan Bobo asked the pig.

“Oink! Oink!” the pig squealed.

“All right,” said Juan Bobo.

Juan Bobo brushed the pig's teeth
with Mama's toothbrush.
Then he got Mama's new dress.
"This dress is too long,"
said Juan Bobo.
He ripped the dress in half.

He put the top half on the pig.

"Oink! Oink!" the pig squealed.

"Wait!" said Juan Bobo.

"You cannot go out like that.

You need a mantilla.

Mama always wears a mantilla

on her head to go to church."

Juan Bobo could not find a mantilla.

But he did find a hammock.

He tied the hammock

around the pig's head.

"You look very pretty," he said.

"But not pretty enough for church."

Juan Bobo put high-heeled shoes
on the pig's feet.
He put earrings on her ears,
and he powdered her face
until it was all white.

Then Juan Bobo dumped a bottle
of perfume over the pig.
"Now you will smell good in church."
Juan Bobo put four dimes
in a handkerchief.
He put the handkerchief
under the pig's dress.
"Mama takes money to church,"
Juan Bobo told the pig.
"You should too.
Now, go!" said Juan Bobo.
"Or you will be late."

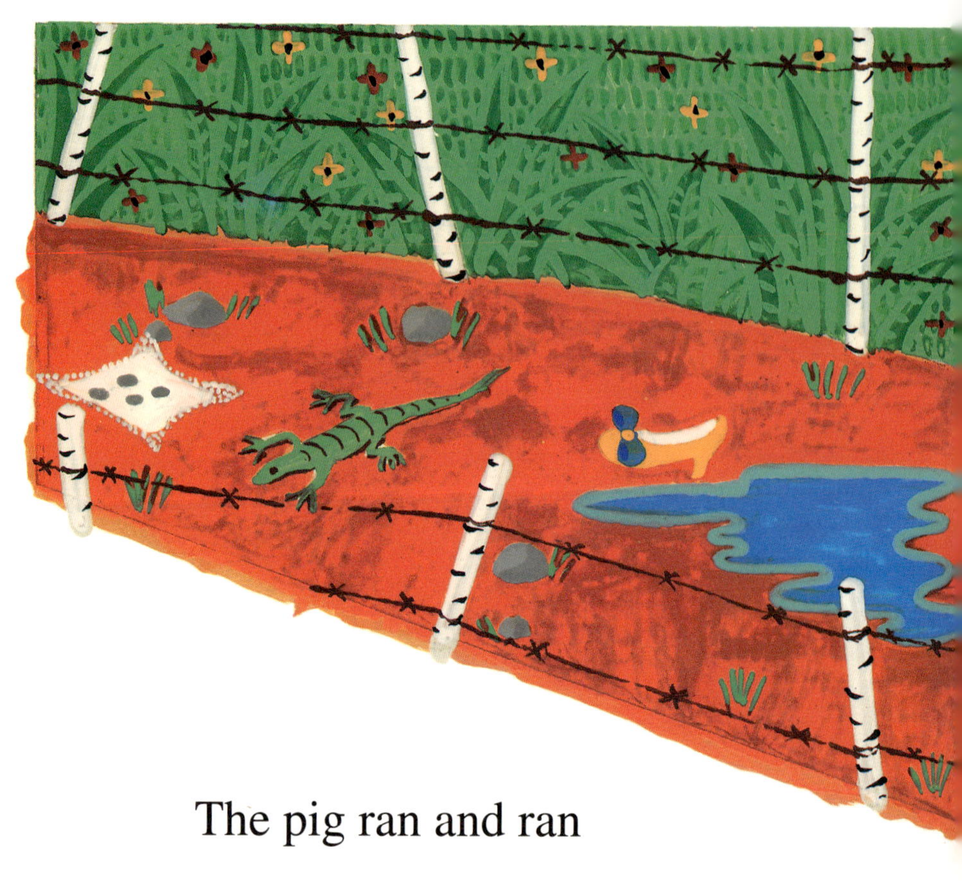

The pig ran and ran

until she came to a puddle.

Then she stopped

and rolled in the mud.

She tore the dress.

She lost the earrings.

Her mantilla flew in the air.

Mama found the pig
on her way home from church.
She grabbed the squealing pig
and dragged her home.

By the time they got home,

Mama was covered with mud.

She was too angry to speak.

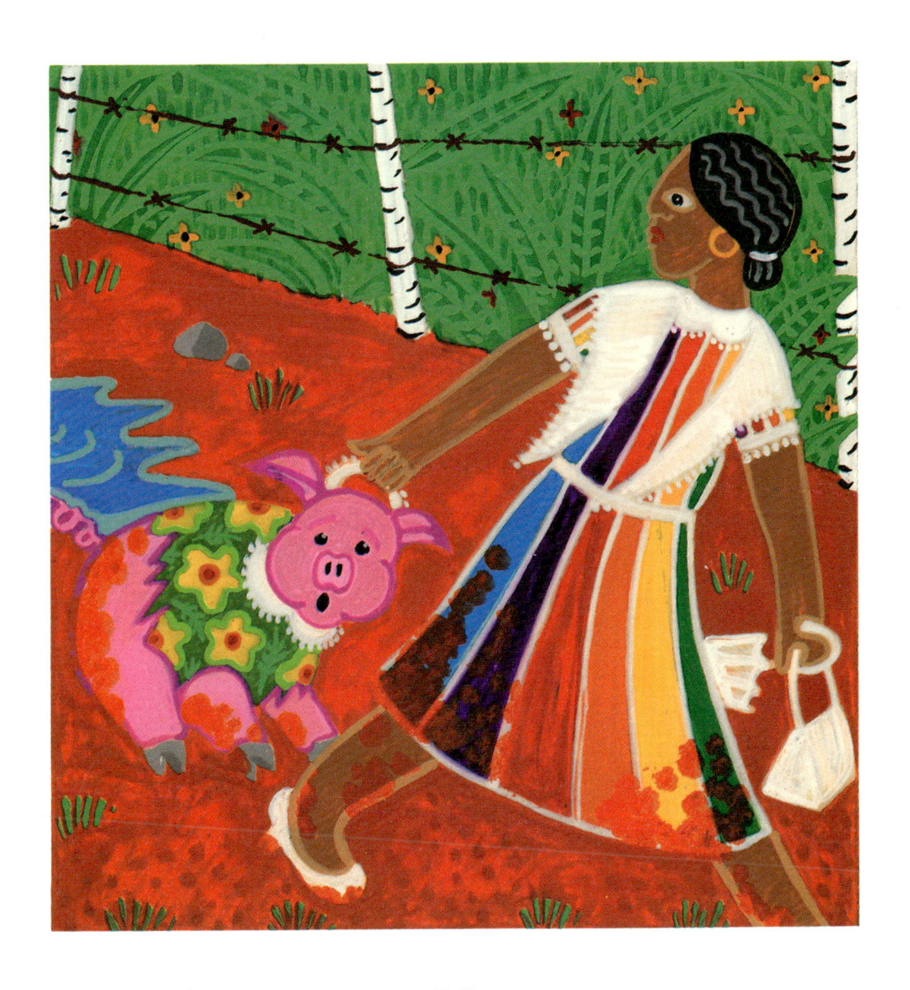

Juan Bobo stared at Mama.

He stared at the pig.

He scratched his head.

Then he smiled.

"Mama!" Juan Bobo said.

"I did not know

you could play with mud in church.

Next Sunday,

I want to go to church too!"

Do Not Sneeze, Do Not Scratch . . . Do Not Eat!

"Juan Bobo," said Mama,

"put on your best clothes.

We are going to visit Señora Soto."

"Who is Señora Soto?"

asked Juan Bobo.

"She is the lady I met last week.
She invited us to eat at her house.
But remember, Juan Bobo,"
Mama warned him,
"do not sneeze
and do not scratch at the table.
And," Mama added,
"when I put my foot on your foot,
stop eating."
"Why?" asked Juan Bobo.
"Because it is not good manners
to eat too much," said Mama.
"Okay, okay," said Juan Bobo.

Soon Juan Bobo and Mama were sitting

at Señora Soto's dining table.

"Rice and beans, Juan Bobo?"

asked Señora Soto.

Juan Bobo put his nose right over
the plate of rice and beans.
"Mmm! It smells good!"
thought Juan Bobo.
He took another big sniff.
But this time he sniffed up
two grains of rice into his nose.
"Ay!" thought Juan Bobo.
"I need to sneeze."
He covered his nose.
He shook his head from side to side.
The two grains of rice fell out.
The sneeze went away.

"So, you do not like

my rice and beans, eh?"

said Señora Soto.

"Juan Bobo! Manners!" said Mama.

"That is okay," said Señora Soto.

And she took the plate away.

When she returned, Señora Soto asked,

"Steak, Juan Bobo?"

"Yes, please!" Juan Bobo said.

"I have never had a steak."

Señora Soto placed a steak

on Juan Bobo's plate.

"What do you say?"

Mama asked.

"Thank you," said Juan Bobo.

"Remember your manners,"

said Mama.

"Do not touch the steak

with your hands."

Juan Bobo picked up the steak

with a big spoon.

But before he could take a bite,

the steak fell off the spoon

and onto his lap.

Juan Bobo started

to pick up the steak.

Then he remembered Mama had said,

“Do not touch the steak

with your hands.”

So he put his hands

back on the table.

When Señora Soto returned,
she said, "Juan Bobo!
You ate the whole steak!
Now you can have fried bananas."
Juan Bobo forgot
all about the steak.
He loved fried bananas!
But when Señora Soto passed
the fried bananas,
a mosquito bit
Juan Bobo's neck.

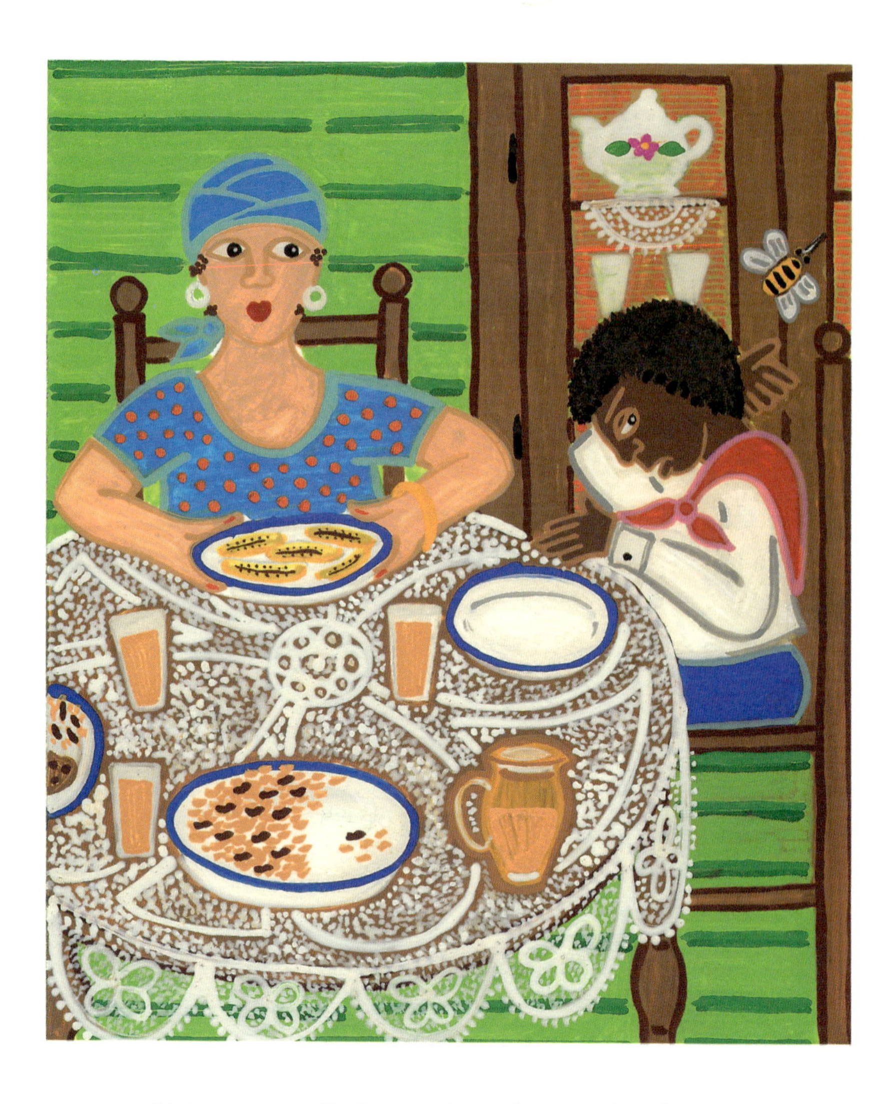

“Ay, no!” Juan Bobo cried out

as he rubbed his neck

against the back of the chair.

"No thank you, Juan Bobo,"

Mama corrected.

"No bananas?"

Señora Soto said.

"I guess you are saving room

for ice cream."

She gave Juan Bobo ice cream.

"What do you say?"

Mama asked.

"Thank you, Señora Soto,"

said Juan Bobo.

But when Juan Bobo opened his mouth

to eat some ice cream,

the steak fell on his foot.

"Why is Mama putting her foot

on mine?" Juan Bobo wondered.

"I did not eat anything!"

Juan Bobo kicked.

"Mama!" he shouted.

"Take your foot off my foot!

“If good manners means no eating,

I have had enough good manners.

I am going home!”

Juan Bobo stood up so quickly,

he tipped over the table!

And he ran home

with a very empty stomach.

A Dime a Jug

"Juan Bobo!" Mama scolded.

"Stop tasting that sugarcane syrup,

or you are going to pay for it."

Mama put corks in the jugs.

"Go sell this syrup to the widows,"

she told Juan Bobo.

"Ask them for a dime a jug."

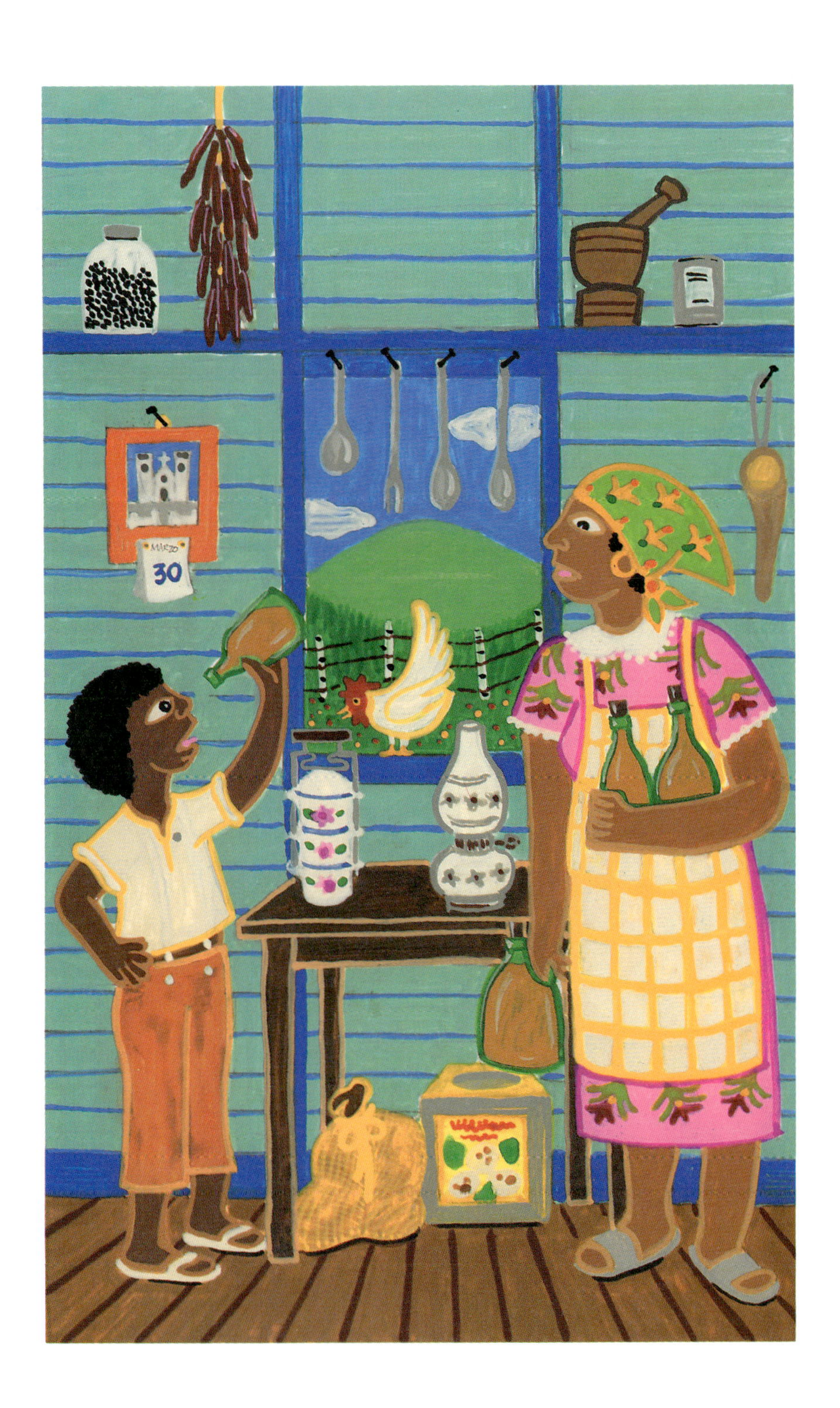
MARZO
30

"Who are the widows?"
Juan Bobo asked.
"They are the ones
who will be coming
out of church soon," Mama said.
"They wear shiny black dresses
and carry fans.
They are small,
and they speak softly."
"All right," said Juan Bobo.
He grabbed the jugs and left.

MELAO

On the way to church
Juan Bobo saw a handkerchief
lying in the mud.
He picked up the handkerchief.
Out popped four dimes!
"What luck!" said Juan Bobo.
He put the dimes in his pocket
and kept walking.
But when he walked around
a big mud puddle,
he took the wrong path.

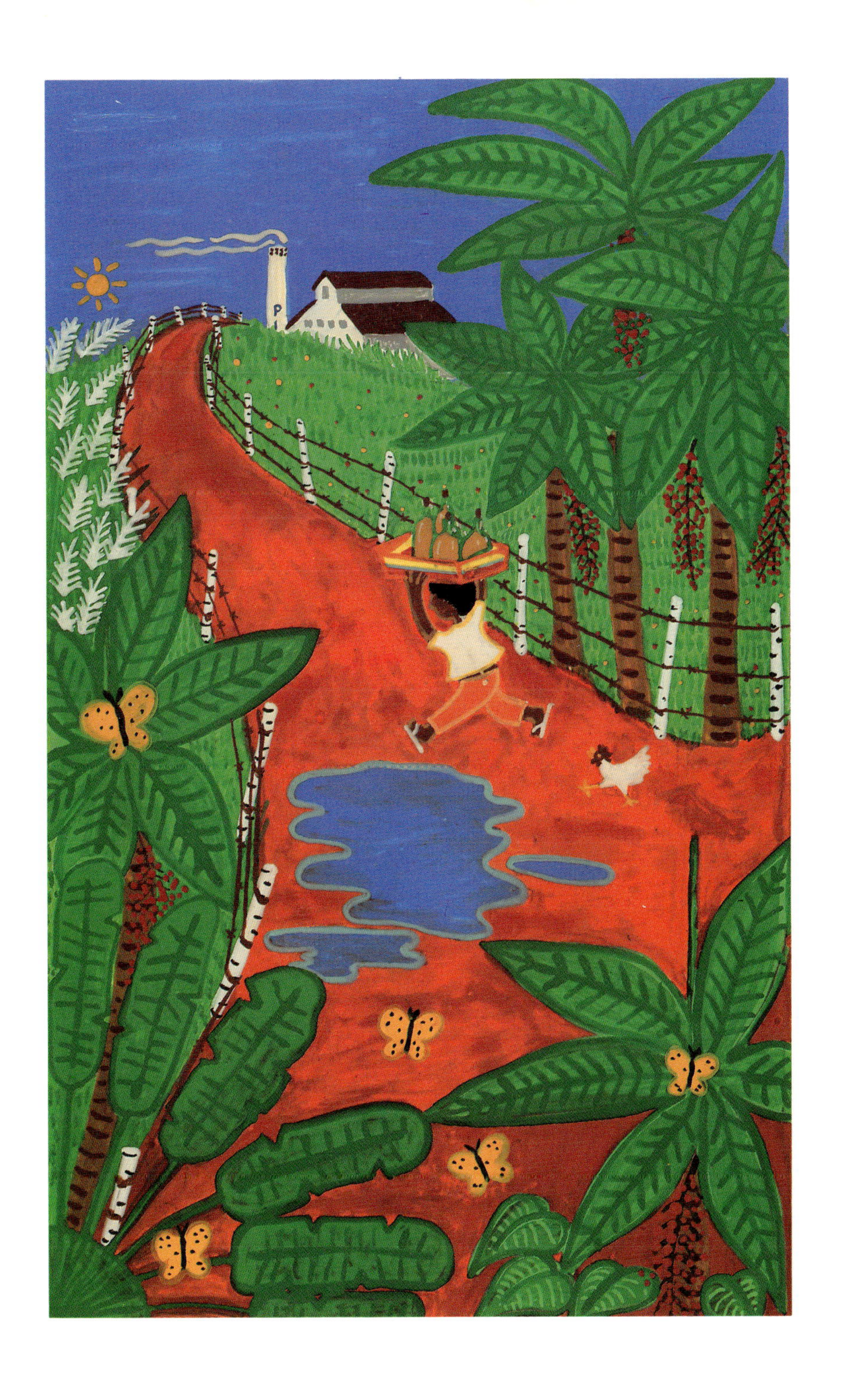

After hours of walking

up one hill

and down the next,

he came to a sugar mill.

“That is the church!”

Juan Bobo thought.

“Syrup! Delicious syrup!” he cried.

Four flies flew out of the mill.

"Shiny black dresses!"

Juan Bobo thought.

He saw the flies' wings.

"Fans!" he thought.

The flies flew closer.

"They are small,"

Juan Bobo told himself.

He heard the flies buzz.

"And they speak softly.

They must be the widows!"

"Syrup!" Juan Bobo called.

"A dime a jug!"

But the flies just flew

around and around the jugs.

"All right," Juan Bobo said.

"I will open the jugs for you."

He pulled out the corks.

The flies flew into the jugs.

"Stop!" yelled Juan Bobo.

“Stop tasting that syrup,

or you are going to pay for it!”

But the flies did not stop.

Juan Bobo had to shake them

out of the jugs.

The flies began to fly away.

“Wait!” Juan Bobo yelled.

"You have to pay for your syrup!"

Juan Bobo started to run after them,

but he tripped and fell.

The four dimes

popped out of his pocket.

Juan Bobo saw the dimes

on the ground.

"They paid!" Juan Bobo said.

Then he remembered the jugs.

"Hey! Widows!"

Juan Bobo called.

"You forgot your syrup."

But the flies flew into the mill.

PLATA

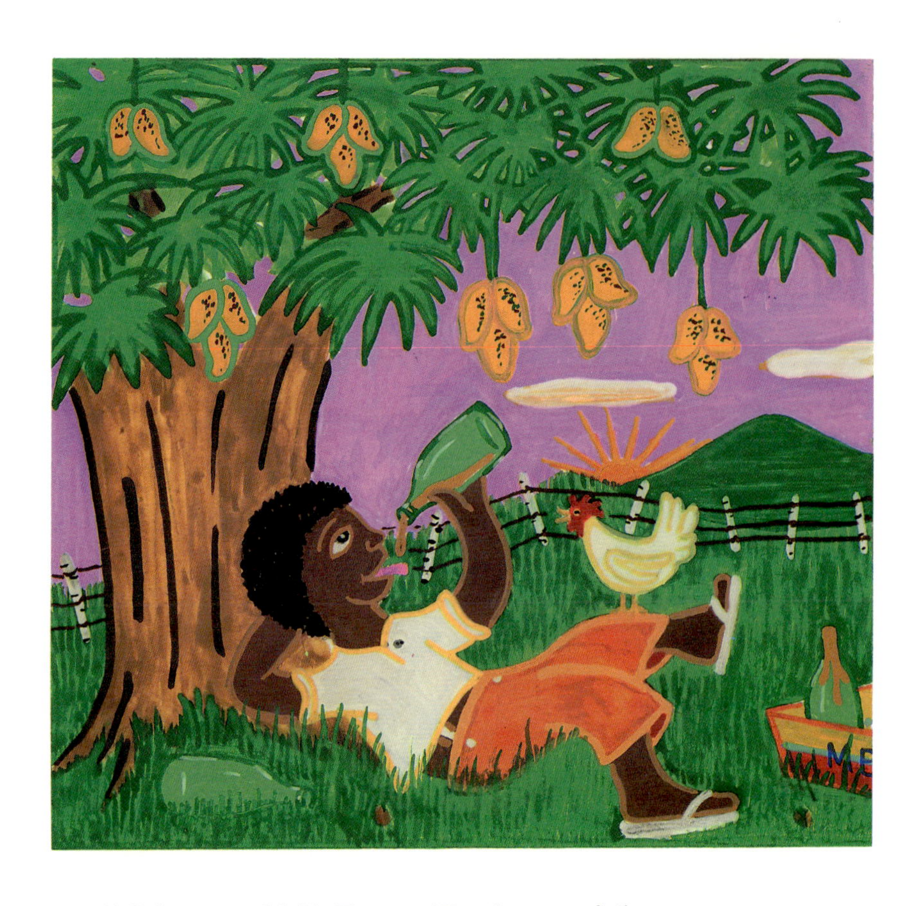

“Oh, well,” Juan Bobo said.

“If they do not like syrup, I do.”

He sat down and drank all the syrup.

He left the empty jugs

for the widows.

It was dark when Juan Bobo got home.

He gave Mama the four dimes.

"I sold the jugs of syrup," he said.

Mama hugged him.

"Tonight, Juan Bobo,

you can eat

as much

as you want!"

"No thank you,

Mama,"

said Juan Bobo.

"Tonight

I am

very full!"

And off

to bed

he went.

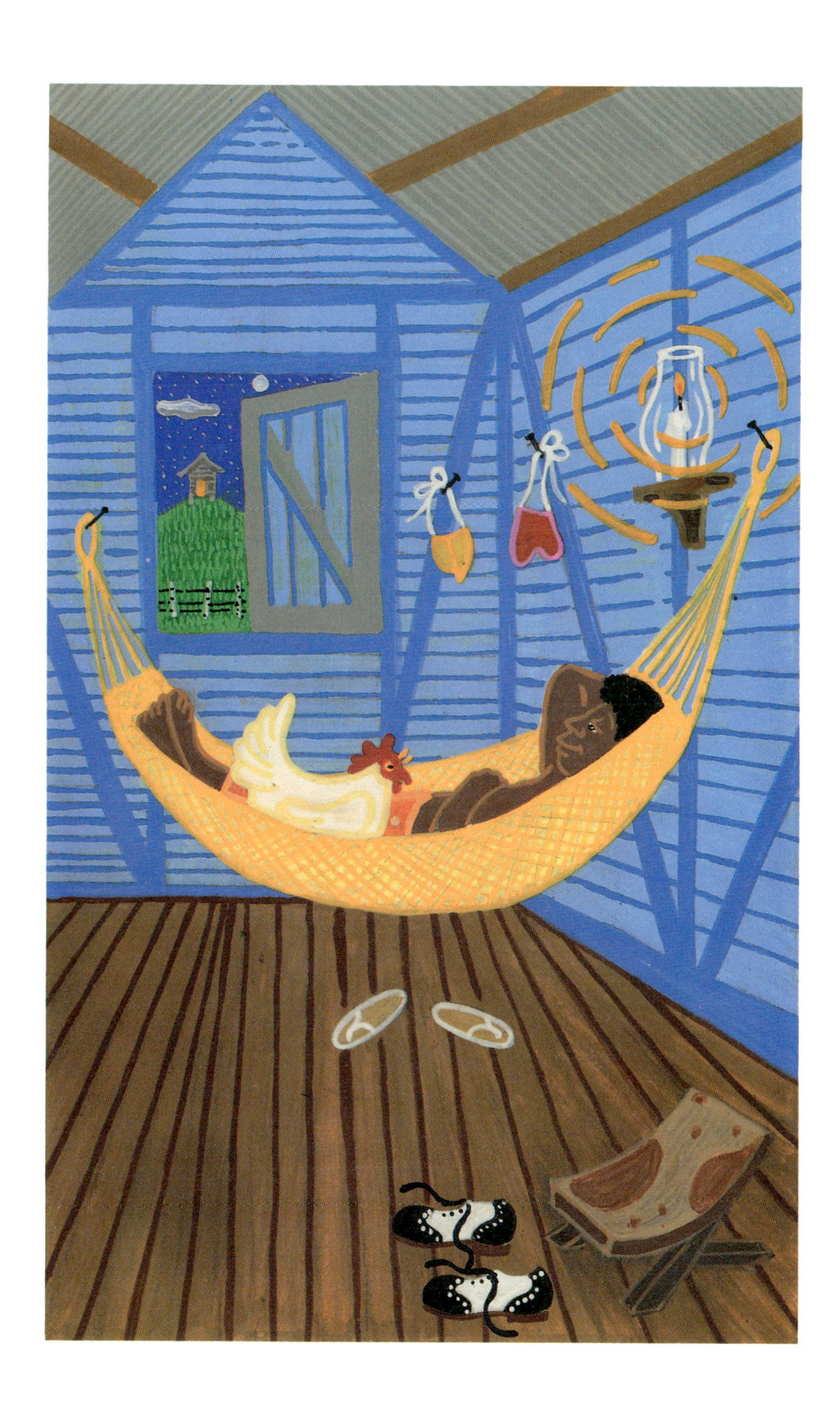

La mejor manera de cargar agua

—¡Juan Bobo! —Mamá llamó.
—Sí, Mamá —dijo Juan Bobo.
—Por favor, traéme agua del río —dijo Mamá.
—¡Ay! —lloriqueó Juan Bobo—. ¿Tengo que traérla?
Mamá dejó caer dos baldes vacíos fuera de la puerta.
—Necesito agua para lavar los platos —dijo.
—Ay, Mamá —dijo Juan Bobo—. Esos baldes pesan mucho cuando están llenos.
—Entonces usa otra cosa —dijo Mamá—, pero traéme agua.
—Ay —dijo Juan Bobo.
Mamá barrió y sacudió el polvo en la sala y el dormitorio. Entonces regresó a la cocina.
—¿Juan Bobo, me trajiste el agua? —preguntó.
—Sí, Mamá —dijo Juan Bobo—. Y adivina qué, Mamá. Yo creo que me estoy poniendo más fuerte.
—¿Por qué? —dijo Mamá.
—Porque —dijo Juan Bobo—, según yo iba caminando de regreso del río, el agua se sentía más y más liviana.
—Eso es muy extraño —dijo Mamá.
Entonces ella pisó un gran charco.
—¡Juan Bobo! ¿Es esta el agua que me trajiste?
—¡No, Mamá! —dijo Juan Bobo—. El agua que yo te traje está en esas dos canastas.

Una cerda en ropa de domingo

—Juan Bobo —Mamá dijo—. O vas a la iglesia conmigo o cuidas a la cerda.
—Cuidaré a la cerda, Mamá.
Tan pronto Mamá se fue para la iglesia, la cerda comenzó a chillar.
—¿Quieres ir a la iglesia? —Juan Bobo le preguntó a la cerda.
—¡Pru-pru! ¡Pru-pru! —la cerda chilló.
—Está bien —dijo Juan Bobo.
Juan Bobo cepilló los dientes de la cerda con el cepillo de dientes de Mamá. Después cogió el vestido nuevo de Mamá.
—Este vestido está muy largo —dijo Juan Bobo. Rasgó el vestido por la mitad. Le puso la parte de arriba a la cerda.
—¡Pru-pru! ¡Pru-pru! —la cerda chilló.
—¡Espérate! —dijo Juan Bobo—. No te puedes ir así. Necesitas

una mantilla. Mamá siempre usa una mantilla en la cabeza para ir a la iglesia.

Juan Bobo no pudo encontrar una mantilla. Pero sí encontró una hamaca. Él le ató la hamaca a la cabeza.

—Te ves muy bonita —dijo—. Pero no lo bastante bonita para ir a la iglesia.

Juan Bobo le puso zapatos de tacones a las patas de la cerda. Le puso aretes a sus orejas y le empolvó la cara hasta que quedó toda blanca.

Entonces Juan Bobo vació una botella de perfume sobre la cerda.

—Ahora olerás bien en la iglesia.

Juan Bobo puso cuatro monedas de diez centavos en un pañuelo. Colocó el pañuelo debajo del vestido.

—Mamá lleva dinero a la iglesia —Juan Bobo le dijo a la cerda—. Tú también debes de llevarlo.

—¡Véte ahora! —dijo Juan Bobo—. O llegarás tarde.

La cerda corrió y corrió hasta que llegó a un charco. Entonces se detuvo y se revolvió en el lodo. Ella desgarró el vestido. Perdió los aretes. Su mantilla voló por el aire.

Mamá encontró a la cerda en su camino de regreso de la iglesia. Agarró a la cerda y la arrastró chillando a la casa.

Cuando llegaron a la casa, Mamá estaba cubierta de lodo. Ella tenía tanto coraje que no pudo hablar.

Juan Bobo clavó los ojos en Mamá. Fijó su vista en la cerda. Se rascó la cabeza y sonrió.

—¡Mamá! —Juan Bobo dijo—. Yo no sabía que se podía jugar con lodo en la iglesia. El próximo domingo, ¡yo también quiero ir a la iglesia!

¡No estornudes, no te rasques . . . no comas!

—Juan Bobo —dijo Mamá—, ponte tu mejor ropa. Vamos a visitar a la Señora Soto.

—¿Quién es la Señora Soto? —preguntó Juan Bobo.

—Es la señora que conocí la semana pasada. Nos invitó a comer a su casa. Pero acuérdate, Juan Bobo —Mamá le advirtió—, no estornudes y no te rasques en la mesa.

—Y —Mamá añadió—, cuando yo ponga mi pie sobre tu pie, deja de comer.

—¿Por qué? —preguntó Juan Bobo.

—Porque comer demasiado no es de buenos modales —dijo Mamá.
—Está bien, está bien —dijo Juan Bobo.
Al rato Juan Bobo y Mamá estaban sentados en la mesa del comedor de la Señora Soto.
—¿Arroz con habichuelas, Juan Bobo? —preguntó la Señora Soto.
Juan Bobo colocó su nariz sobre el plato de arroz con habichuelas.
—¡Mmm! ¡Huele bien! —pensó Juan Bobo.
Él volvió a olfatear, pero más fuerte. Esta vez, dos granos de arroz se le metieron por la nariz.
—¡Ay! —pensó Juan Bobo—. Necesito estornudar.
Se cubrió la nariz. Movió la cabeza de lado a lado. Los dos granos se salieron. El estornudo se ahuyentó.
—¿Así que no te gusta mi arroz con habichuelas, ah? —dijo la Señora Soto.
—¡Juan Bobo! ¡Modales! —dijo Mamá.
—Está bien —dijo la Señora Soto. Y se llevó el plato.
Cuando la Señora Soto regresó, preguntó:
—¿Filete, Juan Bobo?
—¡Sí, por favor! —Juan Bobo dijo—. Yo nunca he comido filete.
La Señora Soto puso un filete en el plato de Juan Bobo.
—¿Qué se dice? —Mamá preguntó.
—Gracias —dijo Juan Bobo.
—Recuerda tus modales —dijo Mamá—. No toques el filete con las manos.
Juan Bobo cogió el filete con una cuchara grande. Pero antes de que pudiese tomar un bocado, el filete se cayó de la cuchara a su falda. Juan Bobo fue a recoger el filete.
Entonces recordó lo que Mamá había dicho:
—No toques el filete con las manos.
Así es que él subió sus manos otra vez a la mesa.
Cuando la Señora Soto regresó, dijo:
—¡Juan Bobo! ¡Te comistes todo el filete! Ahora puedes comer tostones.
A Juan Bobo se le olvidó el filete. ¡A él le encantaban los tostones!
Pero cuando la Señora Soto pasó los tostones, un mosquito le picó el cuello de Juan Bobo.
—¡Ay, no! —Juan Bobo gritó,

frotándose el cuello con el espaldar.
—No gracias, Juan Bobo — Mamá corrigió.
—¿No quieres tostones? —la Señora Soto dijo—. Me imagino que estás esperando por el helado.
Ella le dió helado a Juan Bobo.
—¿Qué se dice? —preguntó Mamá.
—Gracias, Señora Soto —dijo Juan Bobo.
Pero cuando Juan Bobo abrió la boca para comerse el helado, el filete le cayó al pie.
—¿Por qué Mamá está poniendo su pie en el mío? —Juan Bobo se preguntó. —¡Yo no he comido nada!
Juan Bobo pateó.
—¡Mamá! —gritó—. ¡Saca tu pie de mi pie!
Si tener buenos modales quiere decir que no puedo comer, ya yo he tenido bastante buenos modales. ¡Me voy a casa!
Juan Bobo se levantó tan rápido que ¡volteó la mesa¡
Y corrió a la casa con un estómago muy vacío.

Diez centavos la jarra

—¡Juan Bobo! —Mamá riñó—. Deja de probar el guarapo de caña o tendrás que pagar por él.
Mamá tapó con corchos las jarras.
—Ve a vender este guarapo a las viudas —ella le dijo a Juan Bobo—. Pídeles diez centavos por jarra.
—¿Quiénes son las viudas? —Juan Bobo preguntó.
—Ellas son las que están por salir pronto de la iglesia —Mamá dijo—. Ellas se visten con vestidos negros brillantes y cargan abanicos. Son pequeñas y hablan suavemente.
—Está bien —dijo Juan Bobo.
Cogió las jarras y se fue.
En el camino hacia la iglesia, Juan Bobo vió un pañuelo tirado en el lodo. Él recogió el pañuelo.
¡Del pañuelo saltaron cuatro monedas de diez centavos!
—¡Qué suerte! —dijo Juan Bobo.
Guardó las monedas en su bolsillo y siguió caminando. Pero al caminar alrededor de un lodazal, tomó el camino erróneo.
Después de estar horas caminando, subiendo una colina y bajando la próxima, se encontró con un molino de azúcar.
—¡Esa es la iglesia! —Juan Bobo pensó.

—¡Guarapo! ¡Delicioso guarapo! —gritó.
Cuatro moscas volaron fuera del molino.
—¡Vestidos negros brillantes! —Juan Bobo pensó.
Él vió las alas de las moscas.
—¡Abanicos! —pensó.
Las moscas volaron más cerca.
—Son pequeñas —Juan Bobo se dijo a sí mismo.
Las oyó zumbar.
—Y hablan suavemente. ¡Esas deben de ser las viudas!
—¡Guarapo! —Juan Bobo gritó—. ¡Diez centavos la jarra!
Pero las moscas sólo volaron alrededor y alrededor de las jarras.
—Está bien —Juan Bobo dijo—. Les voy a abrir las jarras.
Él sacó los corchos. Las moscas volaron al interior de las jarras.
—¡Deténganse! —gritó Juan Bobo—.
¡Dejen de probar el guarapo o tendrán que pagar por él!
Pero las moscas no se detuvieron. Juan Bobo tuvo que sacudirlas fuera de las jarras. Las moscas empezaron a volar lejos.
—¡Esperen! —Juan Bobo gritó—. ¡Ustedes tienen que pagarme por su guarapo!
Juan Bobo empezó a correr detrás de ellas pero tropezó y se cayó. Las cuatro monedas saltaron fuera de su bolsillo. Juan Bobo vió las monedas en el suelo.
—¡Pagaron! —Juan Bobo dijo.
Entonces se acordó de las jarras.
—¡Oigan! ¡Viudas! —Juan Bobo llamó—. Se les olvidó el guarapo.
Pero las moscas volaron al molino.
—Bueno —Juan Bobo dijo—. Si a ellas no les gusta el guarapo, a mí sí me gusta.
Él se sentó y se tomó todo el guarapo. Él le dejó las jarras vacías a las viudas.
Estaba oscuro cuando Juan Bobo llegó a la casa. Él le dió las cuatro monedas de diez centavos a Mamá.
—Vendí las jarras de guarapo —dijo.
Mamá lo abrazó.
—¡Esta noche, Juan Bobo, puedes comer todo lo que quieras!
—No, gracias, Mamá —dijo Juan Bobo—. Esta noche me siento muy lleno.
Y a dormir se fue.

V9-AFY-293

STARTING SCIENCE

SOUND AND MUSIC

KAY DAVIES
AND
WENDY OLDFIELD

STECK-VAUGHN
LIBRARY
A Division of Steck-Vaughn Company
Austin, Texas

Starting Science

Books in the series

Animals
Electricity and Magnetism
Floating and Sinking
Food
Light
Sound and Music
Waste
Weather

About This Book

Sound and Music investigates, in relation to children's early experiences, how sound is produced, transmitted, and received. The themes develop children's aural skills through sound recognition, dynamics, and pitch variation. They learn that sounds can be produced naturally and mechanically, and also how sound can make music and be useful in other ways.

This book provides an introduction to methods in scientific inquiry and recording. The activities and investigations are designed to be straightforward but fun, and flexible according to the abilities of the children.

The main picture and its commentary may be taken as an introduction to the topic or as a focal point for further discussion. Each chapter can form a basis for extended topic work.

Teachers and parents will find that in using this book, they are reinforcing the other core subjects of language and mathematics. By means of its topical approach ***Sound and Music*** covers aspects of the following subjects which are usually taught in the early grades—exploration of science, types and uses of materials, the scientific aspects of information technology and microelectronics, and sound and music.

Editors: Cally Chambers, Susan Wilson

Typeset by Multifacit Graphics, Keyport, NJ
Printed in Italy by Rotolito Lombarda S.p.A., Milan
Bound in the U.S. by Lake Book, Melrose Park, IL
1 2 3 4 5 6 7 8 9 0 LB 96 95 94 93 92

Library of Congress
Cataloging-in-Publication Data

Davies, Kay.
Sound and music / Kay Davies and Wendy Oldfield.
p. cm. -- (Starting science)
Includes index.
Summary: Focuses on how sound is produced, transmitted, and received. Activities explore aural skills through sound recognition, dynamics, and pitch variation.
ISBN 0-8114-3003-0
1. Sound--Juvenile literature. 2. Sound--Experiments--Juvenile literature. 3. Music--Acoustics and physics--Juvenile literature. [1. Sound 2. Sound--Experiments. 3. Experiments.] I. Oldfield, Wendy. II. Title. III. Series: Davies, Kay. Starting science.
QC225.5.D39 1992 91-23475
534--dc20 CIP AC

CONTENTS

Words that first appear in **bold** in the text or captions are explained in the glossary.

These drummers play the drums with their hands.
The rhythm makes us want to dance.

BEAT THE DRUM

You can use an empty cookie can or coffee can to make your own drum.

Stretch a piece of plastic wrap over the can like a tight skin. Make sure that the edges are sealed.

Tap out a **rhythm** on your drum with your fingers or a stick.

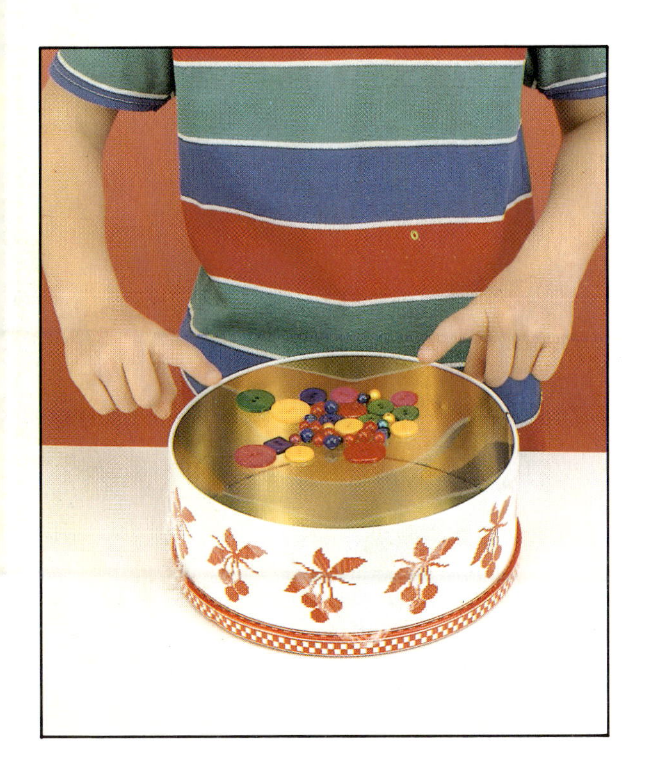

Put some buttons and beads on the plastic wrap.

Now tap your drum and watch them jump.

The skin shakes the air too, just like it shakes the buttons and beads.

All the sounds you hear are made when the air shakes or **vibrates**.

WHAT'S THAT SOUND?

We hear sounds with our ears. We can learn to tell one sound from another.

Find some objects like these and play a sound game with your friends.

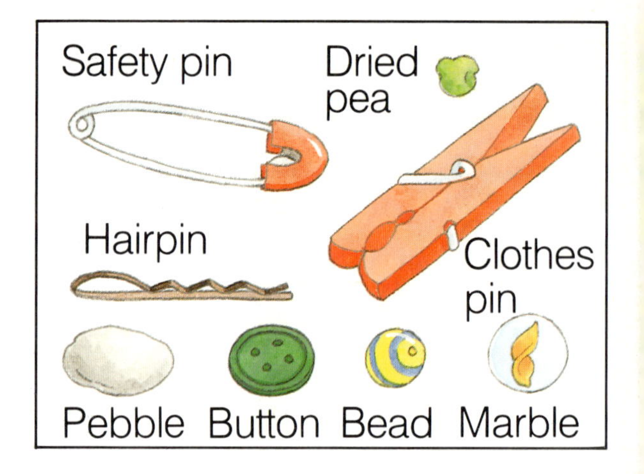

Put each object, one at a time, into a box. Shake it and listen carefully to the sound. Now take turns. Put an object in the box while your friends close their eyes.

Shake the box while the others listen. Can they guess what is making the sound?

The market is full of busy people buying their food.
There are noises all around.

The rattlesnake shakes its tail. The rattling noise warns people and animals to keep away.

SHAKE AND RATTLE

We can make rattling sounds like the rattlesnake.

Put some pebbles in a can. Shake your can and listen to the loud sounds.

Put some sand in another can. Shake your can and listen to the soft sounds.

Try objects like marbles, buttons, rice, beans, sugar, crayons, and paper clips in your can. Test which make loud sounds and which make soft sounds.

Make different rattles with your objects.

Try using a glass jar, a plastic cup, a paper bag, and a cardboard box.

Do they all sound the same? Try to describe the sounds.

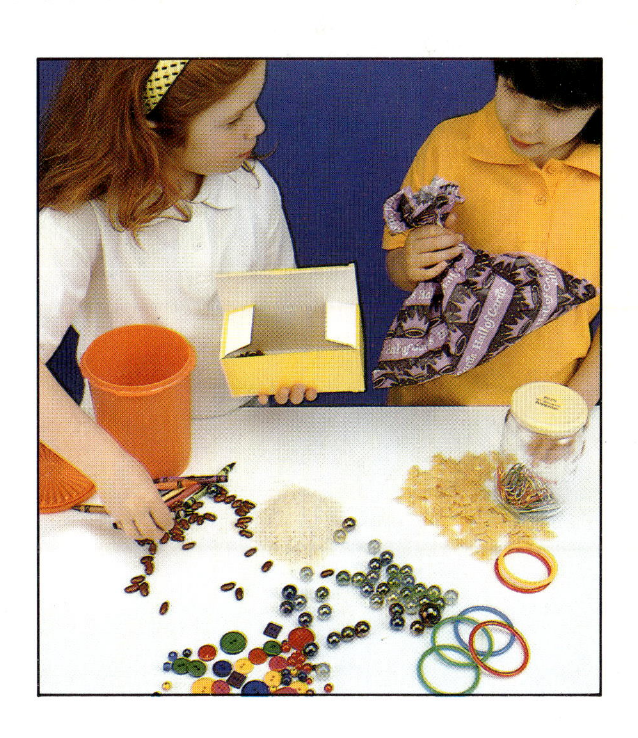

POT AND PAN BAND

A pot and pan band can make lots of sounds.

Make a collection of pans, lids, spoons, and other kitchen things.

Tie them with string and hang them from a pole.

Rest your pole firmly on the backs of two chairs.

Use a wooden spoon to tap all the things. Listen for high sounds and low sounds. Try to put them in order from high to low.

Hit your pots and pans, then hold them to stop them from shaking. What happens to the sounds now?

Music played on the steel drums is fun to listen to.
The drums make high sounds and low sounds.

A GOOD BLOW

Whistles make sounds when we blow into them.

Use a plastic straw to make your own whistle.

Flatten one end and shape it to a point with scissors.

Practice blowing into the pointed end to make a loud sound.

Cut some straws to make whistles of different lengths.

You can blow high sounds with short straws and low sounds with long straws.

You can make panpipes like this. Line your whistles up, from shortest to longest. Glue them together.

The **referee** blows the whistle loudly so that everyone can hear. They stop playing the game.

The harp is a musical instrument with many strings.
We **pluck** the strings with our fingers to play tunes.

LOTS OF PLUCK

String, **wire**, or elastic can be pulled tight and plucked with your fingers.

The wire strings on this guitar vibrate and make music.

Plucking long strings makes low **notes**.

Plucking short strings makes high notes.

You can make your own guitar from a shoebox.

Draw a circle near one end of the lid. Cut it out.

Roll up the circle to make a **bridge** for the strings. Set it at a slant on the lid.

Stretch large rubber bands around the box and lid. Rest the rubber bands on the bridge.

The waves crash onto the beach. The water rattles the stones and shells as it goes back out.

SOUNDS THE SAME

You can copy the sound of waves on a beach.

Put some small stones in a cardboard box. Fill a jar with water and put two straws in it.

Ask a friend to gently roll the box while you blow through the straws.

You can make up a play and use **sound effects**.

A pencil rubbed over a comb sounds like winding a clock or toy. Blocks of wood tapped together sound like footsteps. Blowing across the open top of an empty bottle makes a sound like a ship's whistle.

SOUND AN ALARM

Bells, **sirens**, and whistles can all be used to make alarm and message sounds.

They usually make high, loud sounds. They can be heard clearly from a long way off.

Here are some different alarm and message sounds. Are they bells, sirens, or whistles?

Make a chart of other message sounds. Check off all the ones you have heard.

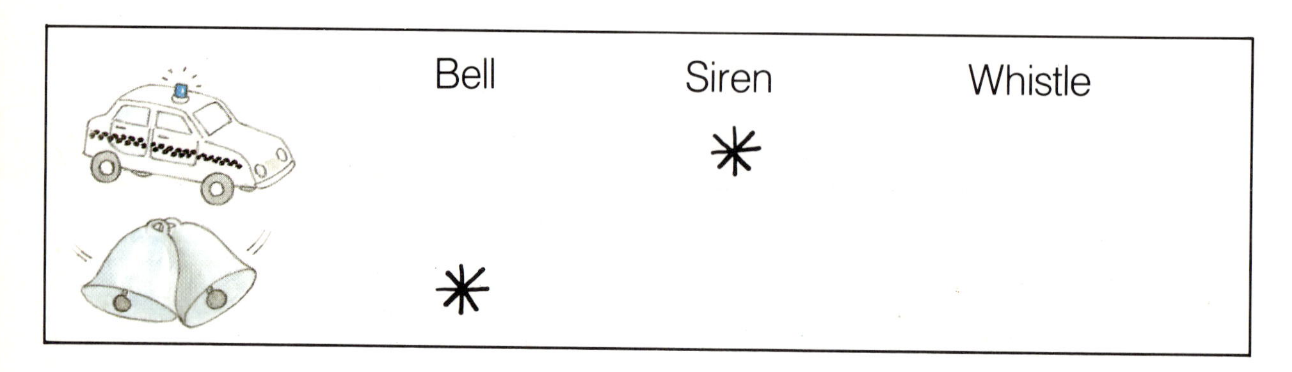

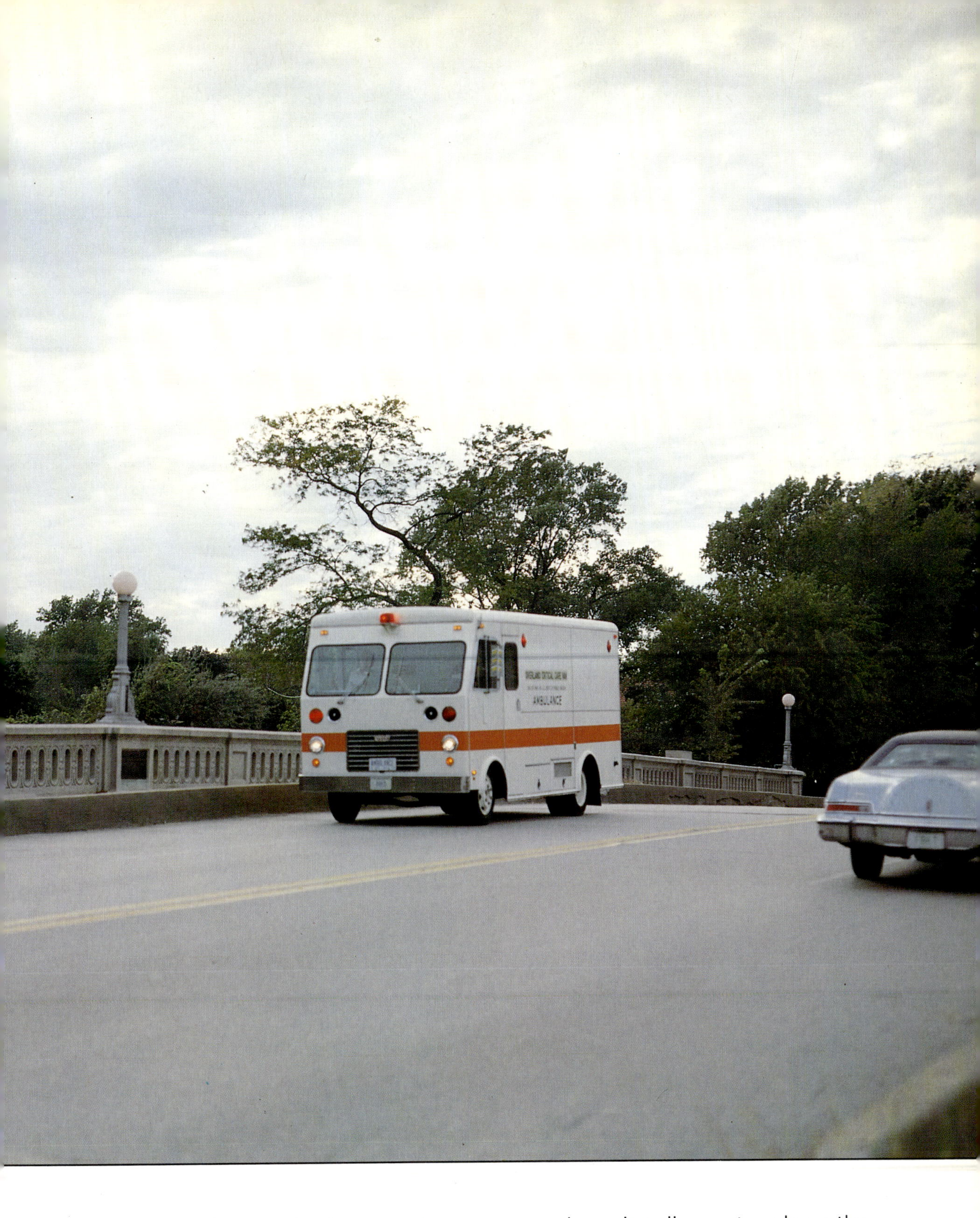

The siren on the ambulance gives a warning. It tells us to clear the road and be careful.

A LOUD VOICE

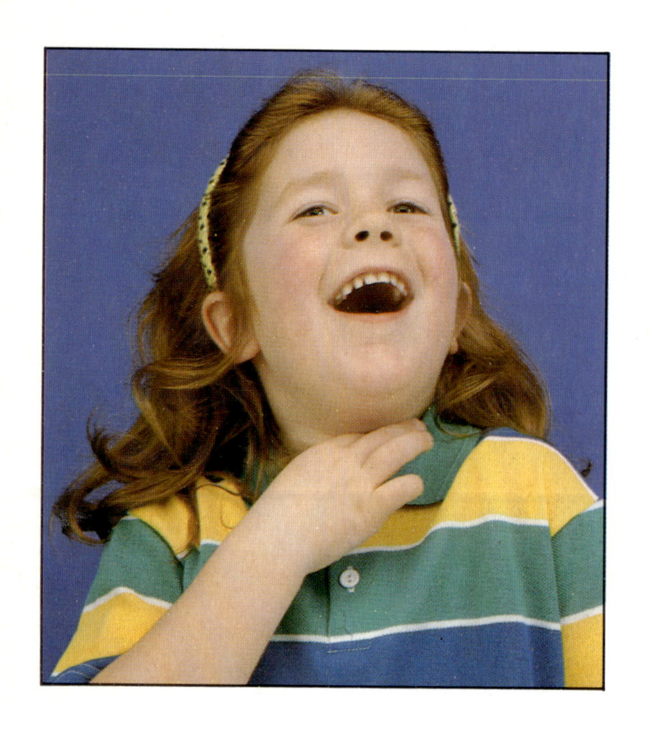

We can feel sounds.

Gently rest your fingers on your throat and talk to a friend.

Then try whispering, shouting, and laughing.

A loud voice makes your throat vibrate more than a soft one.

Speaking through a funnel makes a voice very loud.

Make this **megaphone** with cardboard and tape. Make it open at both ends.

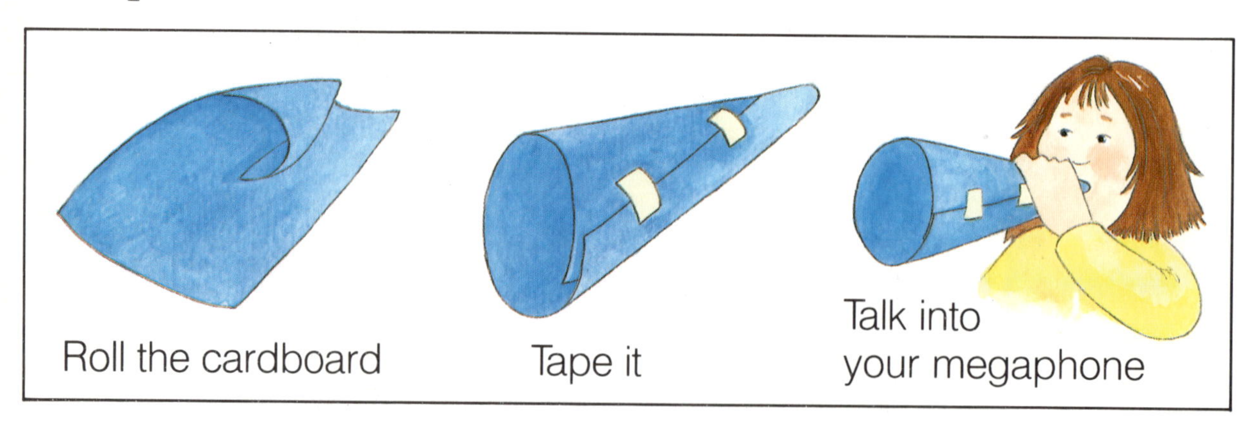
Roll the cardboard
Tape it
Talk into your megaphone

Speak to your friend with your megaphone and then without it. Ask your friend which sounds louder.

The man uses a megaphone to talk to the crowd,
so more people can hear him.

The jackrabbit's big ears collect sounds. It can hear noises from all around.

BIG EARS

If you hold a megaphone to your ear it picks up sound. It becomes an **ear trumpet**.

Ask a friend to whisper a message so that you can just hear it.

Then use your ear trumpet and see how much louder the message becomes.

Do the test again. Turn your ear trumpet away from your friend's voice. Turn it toward the voice again. Is there any difference?

Look at the shapes of these animals' ears.

They can move their ears to pick up sound from behind and in front.

CAN YOU HEAR ME?

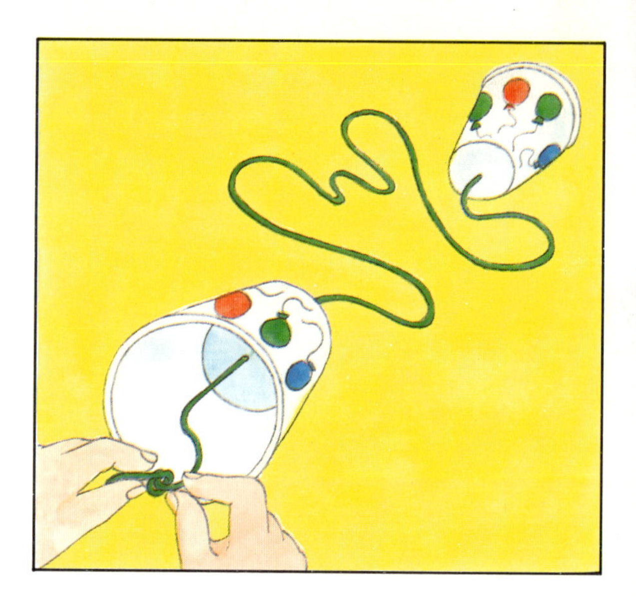

You can make your own telephone.

Use two paper cups and a long piece of string.

Thread the string through a hole in each cup. Tie a knot at each end.

Ask a friend to hold one cup to his or her ear.

Pull the string tight between you.

Speak quietly into the cup. Your friend should hear you clearly.

Can you make a better telephone?

Try different lengths of string, nylon thread, and wire. Try using plastic cups.

Try covering each cup with a piece of plastic wrap. Attach it with a rubber band.

We use the telephone to talk and listen. We can speak to our friends in other towns and countries.

This machine makes a loud noise. **Ear protectors** keep the noise from hurting the woman's ears.

WHAT A DIN!

Some sounds, like noisy machinery or loud music, can hurt your ears.

We need to stop really loud sounds from reaching our ears.

If you expect a loud noise cover your ears with your hands. Do not do what this boy is doing.

We can make places quieter, too.

Put a ticking clock in a metal box or can with a lid. Then put the clock in a cardboard box.

Which sounds louder?

Now put some newspaper in the metal box. Put the clock in and replace the lid. Listen. Can you stop all the sound?

SILENCE

When all is quiet, sit very still and listen. Is there silence or can you hear faraway sounds?

Machines make noises. You may hear cars, a lawn mower, a drill, or a television.

People and animals make noises. You might hear a bird singing, a dog barking, or someone talking. Other things make sounds, too. The wind whistles and the rain drips.

Make a chart of all the noises you hear.

Our world is never really silent.

Even in the quiet of night, your bed might creak and break the silence.

The moon has no air. There are no sounds on the moon.

GLOSSARY

Bridge A support for the strings on a musical instrument.

Ear protectors Pads worn over ears to quiet sounds reaching them.

Ear trumpet A funnel-shaped instrument that collects sound, making it louder.

Megaphone A funnel-shaped instrument that throws out the sound of a voice, making it louder.

Music Lots of notes that are played or sung together.

Note A musical sound.

Pluck To pull and then let go of a string, making it vibrate.

Referee A person who makes sure that players keep to the rules of the game.

Rhythm The pattern of beats in music.

Siren An instrument or machine that makes a loud wailing sound.

Sound effects Sounds made to copy the real thing.

Vibrate To shake up and down quickly.

Wire A long piece of thin metal.

FINDING OUT MORE

Books to read:

Hearing by Henry Pluckrose (Franklin Watts, 1986)
Hearing by J.M. Parramon (Children's Press, 1987)
Music by Carol Greene (Children's Press, 1983)
Musical Instruments by Alan Blackwood (Franklin Watts, 1987)
Sound by Angela Webb (Franklin Watts, 1988)
What's That Noise? by Kate Petty (Franklin Watts, 1986)

PICTURE ACKNOWLEDGMENTS

Cephas Picture Library 11; Chapel Studios 15 top, 26; Eye Ubiquitous 13, 16, 21, 25; Frank Lane Picture Agency 22; Hutchison 4, 7, 12, 14; J. Allan Cash Ltd. 19; Survival Anglia Ltd. 8; Wayland Picture Library (Zul Mukhida) cover, 5 both, 6, 9 both, 10, 15 bottom, 17 both, 20, 23, 24, 27 both; ZEFA 29.
Artwork illustrations by Rebecca Archer. Cover design by Angela Hicks.

INDEX

First published in 1990 by Wayland
(Publishers) Ltd.